BROTHERS
OF THE ZODIAC

FIRE

MAXWELL THOMAS

Cover design © 2018 by Niki Lenhart
nikilen-designs.com

Published by Zarra Knightley Publishing
zarraknightleypublishing.com

ISBN 978-1-946907-32-5 (Trade Paperback)

10 9 8 7 6 5 4 3 2 1

FIRST EDITION

PROLOGUE

TROY
1183 BC

I

AFTER WHAT SEEMED LIKE FOREVER, Gemini and Sagittarius separated from each other while they waited on the banks of the great city of Troy.

"You're still here," said Gemini.

"So are you," noted Sagittarius. "Where did they all go?"

"I don't know. But we're here together."

"Ishtar." Sagittarius walked over to one of the wine skins and took a deep drink. "Ach." He shivered. "Lady Ishtar must have chosen to separate us all."

"What is all this about 'love in another man's eyes' that she said?"

Sagittarius threw the wine skin aside. "Just what it means."

"I have a wife."

"And then, when she dies? Who will you love?"

Gemini frowned. "But I have no interest in men."

Sagittarius sat down at the campfire. "I knew a man like you. A soldier, like you. He loved both women and men. Had a wife, but died loving his lover. Do you love your wife?"

"I haven't seen her in ten years."

He shrugged. "You'll be lucky if she remembers you."

"What about you?"

"I married a few times. But not for love." He tilted his head. "Maybe once for love. But it's a sad thing when the one you love dies and you can't go with them."

Gemini sighed. "I suppose it is."

Sagittarius smiled, reaching down for another wine skin. "If you have no interest in men, then you'll probably live longer."

"What do you mean?"

Sagittarius drank from the wine skin.

"You'll never see love in another man's eyes."

2

Men returned from the city with loot and women, slaves and gold. Troy burned in the distance.

Achilles was dead. Agamemnon had claimed a woman named Cassandra as a slave, who spouted prophecies that were too strange to be believed. The Greeks set the slaves to build boats for the long journey back home.

Gemini, a Greek from a different company than Sagittarius, was absorbed into Sagittarius' unit. The Greeks had lost many men and old companies and units were changed, added to, or completely decimated. They were two of the few that did not have prizes of war, and were looked upon as odd — possibly thieves.

Gemini seemed to sense this. Although he was of a lower rank than Sagittarius, he approached him one evening.

"We have no spoils of war," Gemini noted. "Do you want to return to Greece?"

Sagittarius only shrugged. "I have never been East."

"Neither have I. The Persians may accept us."

"Or try to kill us. But we can't die," he said with a smile.

So, they packed their things, and, in the dead of night, began their trek eastward.

3

The man called Libra found himself in a field of clover and heather. It was night, the moon full and bright above his head. The moon wasn't full when they attacked Troy. How much time had passed?

He stared around him, inhaling the scents. Salt water was nearby; he knew that scent all too well. But he was no longer on the beach — someplace inland, where the moonlight shined dark green everywhere.

He wasn't in Troy, he knew that much.

The Goddess who had brought him back to life ... Ishtar? She must have brought him here. But where was *here*?

In Troy, if he headed north, he would eventually reach some semblance of civilization. He assumed that if he headed north, that it could be the same. He took a whiff of the air: a breeze carried the sea scent from the north.

His world was upside down.

Head south? Again, he sniffed the air. He thought he could smell smoke.

That's impossible, he thought. He couldn't see anything, but he walked through the field, heading south. The smell grew stronger.

He crested a hill and saw a village in the distance. He knew from marching in the Army that he wouldn't make it there until sunrise. He continued to walk through the heather, the scent of the night and the flowers seemed to be the only thing that filled his mind. Yet he still thought about Greece. He knew this wasn't Greece: it was too cold. He was heading south, away from the sea, instead of north.

Libra's mother and sisters would wonder where he had gone to. He had survived the war, the sack of the city, and now he was far away from his home. Would they hold a funeral for him? Pay for the mourners to wail and tear their hair? Would they bury an empty box as a symbol of his death?

He had walked for hours, yet he wasn't tired, which was the strangest thing. He walked from when the night was at its darkest, until he could see the morning star heralding the sun, and the sky turn dark blue as Helios' chariot graced the sky.

Libra came out of the field as a cock crowed. People stirred, as he walked down to the middle of the town square. A few men and women came out of some houses, staring at him. He held his hands out and open in a universal gesture that he was unarmed.

"Who are you?" one man asked in a language that Libra didn't know but understood instinctively.

Libra spoke in his native Greek, but the words came out as something else.

"The Judge."

ARIES

FRANCE
JUNE 10, 1944

I

SERGEANT JOHN JOSEPH ARIES SAT NEXT TO A PRIVATE who hugged the wall of the pockmarked building.

"How's it going?" Aries asked casually.

The private stared at him, his eyes wide, gripping his rifle like it was a lifeline. He couldn't have been more than eighteen.

Aries looked down at the young man's chest: PARKINS.

"That good?"

"Sir?"

"I'm just a sergeant," Aries said comfortingly, putting a big meaty paw on the private's arm. "You don't have to 'sir' me to death. Look, kid, you survived the beach. You're in the 1st division; I'm in the 29th. We're here together right now, so we might as well make the best of it." He pulled out a battered pack of cigarettes and offered one to the private, who shook his head.

"What are we waiting for?" asked Aries, glancing over the kid's shoulder.

"Waiting for the Jerries," he said. "They're right down the street."

"Do they see you?"

"No, sir, I don't think so."

"How long have you been waiting here?"

"I don't know, sir."

Aries knew, because he had sent someone to scout near Saint-Lô, and they hadn't come back yet. The colonel was getting twitchy, and when he got twitchy, he started shouting things down. Shit rolls downhill, and Aries got tasked with finding what happened to the ranger party. So, as he always did, instead of delegating it to someone else to do, he did it himself.

"Three hours, son. You've been sitting here for three hours, shitting your pants. The Jerries might be gone by now."

Aries took up his own rifle and hoisted himself up. He stood a full head and shoulders taller than Parkins - even taller right now that the kid cowered. He walked around Parkins, squeezing between the kid and the corner, and fed his rifle around the corner of the building. He shot randomly, then pulled back, waiting for return fire.

There wasn't any.

Aries slowly crept his way around the corner of the building. He soon stood out in full view of anyone who wanted to take a shot at him from far down the street. Not like they could miss him, with his shock of red hair.

"See, kid? You scared them off."

He happened to look down and to his right. An American GI lay there, his eyes grey and lightless, his hand reaching toward Parkins.

Then Aries heard a couple of shots ring out. He felt them hit his back. The shooter was far enough away that the shots didn't throw him into the wall, but one had penetrated his uniform, embedding itself below his skin.

"Dammit," he spat, and turned around.

He saw someone in a uniform run across the street, easily within range. He raised the rifle to his cheek and took aim.

Like shooting birds, he thought to himself, tracking the man, and then firing off a shot just seconds before the man leapt behind a broken-down truck.

"Shit! You rat!" Aries bolted down the street, into the square, heading straight for the truck.

The man behind the truck rose up, gun in hand. But, at seeing the large red-haired American come rushing toward him, he dropped the gun and yelled *"Bitte!"*

Aries didn't stop. In mid-stride, he flipped the gun around so that he could club the man with the gun instead of shooting him. He wanted this Kraut alive. He slammed the butt of the gun against the man's helmet. It clanged against metal, and the German fell sideways, dazed. Aries grabbed the man by the collar of his jacket, yanking him up straight.

"I'll give you *Bitte!*"

He pulled the man out from behind the truck, and literally dragged him by his collar back to the teenager, who stood at the corner of the building, his rifle slack in his hands.

"Cover me, you ass!"

Aries kept walking, pulling the German behind him. He dropped the German at the boy's feet.

"Rope," said Aries, panting.

Parkins looked like a deer in headlights, confused.

"ROPE!" he repeated to the stunned teen. "Find. Some. Rope!"

The kid jumped and dashed around the corner.

He came back a little while later with some thick hemp rope, the kind used to tie up horses.

It would have to do. Making a slip knot, he tied the German's hands together and pulled him to his feet.

"Congratulations, kid," Aries said, giving the young man a pat on the back. "You just got your first prisoner of war. Now go back and bring this guy with you."

"Where are you going?"

"I'll be a few kilometers behind you."

2

Aries claimed the dog tag of the fallen man — a private by his lack of insignia. A little farther away was another fallen GI hunched over an overturned chair in the middle of the street. As he approached the other man, he whispered a prayer, not to God, but to the Lady who had given him this, his second life.

When he finished taking the dog tag of the second man, Aries craned his neck to try and see where the bullet hole in his shirt was. He could see a large spot of blood a couple of inches above his hip. He pulled the uniform sideways saw that it had been torn, but there was very little blood, so it was probably a scratch.

He ducked into the house, then went upstairs and checked in the bathroom. He found the full-length mirror behind the door. He lifted his shirt and looked behind him.

As he expected, the hole had sealed. He only hoped that his body had expended the bullet during the time he ran across the square.

That's how things usually worked with him: whenever he was injured, the foreign body was always pushed out of the same hole it came in. The deeper it tried to go into his body, the more force was needed.

He tucked his undershirt, then his uniform back into his pants. If anyone asked, he'd say he got punctured by a thorn or something just as silly.

The other line across his side near his ribs had also healed, with a bit of light blood on the undershirt. Otherwise, he was fine.

He caught up with the kid about a quarter of the way down the road. Parkins kept poking the German with his rifle, getting him to move faster. Aries kept his distance while they approached camp. Aries made sure they were out in the open.

The kid was heaped with congratulations as Aries walked by him. He watched the MP's take the German away, and kept on walking to the colonel's bivouac. Once he arrived there, he entered without preamble and saluted smartly. "Reporting on Saint-Lô, sir."

"What is it?" said the colonel, flipping through thin papers and scanning them.

"The northwest sector looks clear," he reported. "We found one sniper."

"Did you see the French?"

"No, sir. We followed this road that we're on. I didn't go looking on any other roads."

The colonel put the papers down. "Where's the rangers?"

"Second battalion's here, sir," said a man about half the size of Aries. Was the Army taking kids in nowadays?

"Balkowski?" When the man nodded, the colonel continued. "Get five rangers and send them west. I want to know if the French are going to start the party without us. Because you know they will."

The man saluted and left.

The colonel turned to look at Aries. "Go on, dismissed."

"Yes, sir."

Aries saluted and also left. Next, he had to report to his captain. Not that he didn't want to.

He thought for a moment. Well, that was true. He didn't want to. He didn't want to get yelled at for going himself to find the rangers.

He found his company near an old milk barn. He nodded to some of the men who knew him, and then checked with the first sergeant to make sure that the captain wasn't busy.

"Callahan's in there with him, having dinner," the first sergeant said.

Aries' eyes widened just a bit. He stood up straight. He straightened his tunic and took off his hat, pushing back his hair. He coughed to announce himself in case they were discussing secret plans, then knocked briskly on the door.

"Enter," came Captain Scott's voice.

Aries opened the door and stepped inside. He had hoped to see his CO first, but instead he saw the other man, Captain Charles "Chuck" Callahan. His blue eyes looked up from his food and crinkled when he smiled at Aries. Aries stared at the man, taking in his slight physique, his thickly tousled brown hair, the way the cut of the uniform fit him. He could have stared at him all day. But he tore his eyes away and focused on Captain Eccles Scott: a balding older man with a paunch, not so attractive.

"What is it?" Captain Scott demanded.

"I found the scout for Saint-Lô."

"We sent three."

Aries tucked a hand in his pocket and showed him the two dog tags. "Brought back a POW."

Scott waved his fork. "We don't need them alive. We need them dead!"

"I'm sure," said Callahan firmly, "that right now they're better alive so we have an idea of what we're up against."

"They won't talk. We'll have to put cigarettes in their eyes for that to happen. Damn Krauts."

Aries swayed in his salute.

Callahan opened his mouth for a rebuttal, then studied Aries. "Did you eat, sergeant?"

"No sir, I'm going to go to mess as soon as I'm done here."

There was a pause, then Scott grumbled, "You're done. Dismissed," and he saluted.

Aries saluted also, doing a precision and perfect 180-degree turn and half-marching out the door.

Thank the gods his tunic came low enough to cover his hard-on.

3

After finishing his dinner in the mess tent, it was full dark. He was blessed with cat's eyes to see better at night, so he was able to find his way through the tangle of tents back to his own company. The men were mostly asleep, so he rolled into his cot with a sigh.

"Aries?" came a whisper in the dark.

"Yeah," he replied, and heard someone rustling in the dark.

Aries looked over to see Private Stewart slink out of his cot. As Aries watched the man weave slowly around the cots, his cock started to swell, knowing what was coming. He undid his tunic, and then pulled his shirt off over his head. By the time he had started to undo his pants, Stewart was already there, helping him with them.

They made very little sound as they both undid the button fly on Aries' pants. Aries swallowed a gasp as his huge cock sprang free from his pants, and Stewart gripped it hard, stroking it immediately. Stewart worked on getting Aries' cock slick and wet. Aries sat up on the cot, glancing around to make sure it was safe. Then, when Stewart had gotten him wet enough, Stewart lay on the ground between Aries' cot and another man's.

Aries bore down on Stewart, getting Stewart's shorts off. He guided himself to Stewart's entrance and thrust in.

Stewart, for his part, had grabbed the pillow from Aries' cot and put it over his face, screaming into it. Aries paused, but pushed slowly forward, listening closely for any odd movements.

He started to thrust and pull out and thrust. Stewart swallowed his moans and cries; Aries only breathed heavier — the sound any man makes when he's masturbating. Aries kept going faster and harder.

He heard a person move. He froze, peered over the cot, and saw a man get up. The man followed the row of cots to the main aisle, then pulled open the flap. He stood there for a minute, then the flap closed.

Stewart growled, "C'mon!"

Aries glared down at him, and then pounded into Stewart, shoving the pillow into Stewart's face. If he really wanted it that bad, he was going to get it.

Stewart could still breathe, because he screamed, and shot his load all over himself. When Aries felt the man's ass clench around his own cock. He pushed through the spasms, and, with a small grunt, filled Stewart's channel with his own thick white juices.

Both men panted, and then Aries took the pillow off Stewart's face. Aries pulled himself out and then rolled back onto the cot, using his shirt to wipe off his cock and then pulled up his shorts. Stewart got up just as the tent flap came open. The light didn't reach where he was standing, but he froze like a jackrabbit regardless. The other man went back to his cot. Stewart also went back to his.

4

The next morning, Stewart was at the latrine with Aries. Aries noted Stewart in the pre-dawn light. He was young, easily in his early 20's, skinny and buck-toothed. His hair was slicked back like all kids his age. Aries was not attracted to him in the least, not by day.

"Like last night?"

Aries said, "What about last night?"

Stewart ribbed Aries. "You know."

Aries looked at Stewart. "I don't know what you're talking about."

"Sarge," he whined.

Aries raised an eyebrow. They had already made arrangements when they were stationed in London: Aries would control the relationship — if there was going to be any. They were both buck privates then. But after D-Day, Aries got promoted to sergeant — a full two ranks — for saving three soldiers of Company A on Omaha Beach.

That was, of course, before Captain Callahan showed up on the scene. Thinking of Callahan, and looking at Stewart, Aries knew which way the wind blew ... and it wasn't in Stewart's direction. But if Stewart decided to shoot his mouth off, who would they believe? A private versus a sergeant?

"Get your head on straight or I'll send you to one of those alienists," Aries said. "Because I don't know what you're talking about."

Aries walked away from the latrine and went to muster with the rest of the unit.

5

After a patrol where, thankfully, no men died, Aries returned to the company camp with his men. He found divisional first, and reported in.

"Hey, Sergeant," said Callahan. He was coming in just as Aries was leaving.

Aries stood up straight. "Captain Callahan," Aries said, saluting.

"Don't bother, Aries. You must be exhausted. I know I am."

"Yes, sir, I am."

"I'm going to report in. Wait here for me, would you?"

"Yes, sir." Aries stood by the doorway of the ruined house and waited as he been ordered to. He didn't know what this meant.

Callahan came out soon after. "Thanks, Sergeant."

"You're welcome, Captain."

"Any idea where you're going?"

He looked out into the dark. "Honestly, sir, no."

"We can get lost together, then. Stupid blackouts."

"Yes, sir. We still have the moon to see by."

They walked for a bit when Callahan said, "I hear you're a guardian angel for the company."

"Sir?"

"Whoever leaves with you always comes back. And sometimes you bring more. I understand you brought a POW in yesterday."

"No, sir, that was Parkins from The Red One."

"Not the way Parkins tells it. He's a country boy. He told them how you walked right up to the Jerry and hit him over the head."

Aries turned away with a small grin. "Well, sir, it wasn't quite like that."

"What was it like?"

Aries told him what happened, and the man listened.

"You brought him back, though, Sarge. That's more than what some of these guys will do out there."

"Like Captain Scott," Aries said.

"Luckily, he doesn't get out there much. But his attitude is passed down to some of his men."

"Not me. War has rules, and two are to respect your enemy, and bring back your friends."

"That's a good attitude to have. Too bad you're not in my company, Sergeant. You'd be a First Lieutenant by the end of the campaign."

"No, sir, I like being in the trenches."

"So I've heard."

They stopped at a tent, where the insignia of a silhouetted man astride a horse was outside the tent and a handwritten sign with a big letter "G" tacked up along with it. "This looks like your stop, Sergeant Aries."

"Yes, sir," he said. "Yours must be right next door."

"If there was a logical design to this. But there isn't." Callahan patted Aries on the shoulder. "Have a good night."

Aries took one step and made a decision. "Wait, sir."

Callahan took a step forward, then turned around. "Yes?"

"Let me escort you to your company, sir."

Callahan laughed. "I can find my way in the dark, Sergeant."

"You said I was a guardian angel, didn't you, sir? Besides, I'm not tired right now."

"I don't know how you can't be tired, but all right."

Callahan went to the next tent: it was Company B for the 115th. So began the wild goose chase for Company F of the 116th regiment.

"Where are you from, Captain?"

"Phoebus, Michigan. You?"

Aries had to think fast of what town he put down when he registered for the Army. "Windsor."

"Nice town?"

"It can be pretty nice in the Fall," he lied. He'd never been there, had looked at a map of Virginia and picked it out when he filled out his forms. He was snatched up two hours after he registered - part of the blessings of Ishtar, as he well knew.

They bumped into another man, who told them the 116th was due north more. They ducked between some tents, and they found "F" company.

"Here you are, sir," said Aries. "Safe and sound."

"Thanks to my guardian angel," said Callahan with a laugh. "You sure you can find your way back?"

"Yes, sir, I can. Sleep well, sir."

When Aries walked back, he had a spring in his step. Stewart called his name when he came into the tent, but Aries didn't answer.

6

After the battle for the town of Saint Lô, the division was told to head west toward the city of Brest, and clear out any German resistance on the way. Aries tried to catch Callahan alone again, but both of them were too busy. Oftentimes, they missed each other by minutes, or they would see each other in passing. Aries fell into the routine of sleep, fight, eat, fight, sleep.

Aries had his normal contingent of six men, and it was very late at night. It was hot, he was tired, and he was starving. They found a house that hadn't been looted in the village of Le Chenay and sat down to eat there. Aries had gone outside in the night air to have a smoke, when he saw headlights bobbing their way up the lane. He immediately unhitched his rifle from his shoulder and aimed it at the oncoming vehicle.

He stood at the side of the road. The vehicle's headlights caught him and didn't come directly at him, but pulled over right in front of him.

"Hey, soldier," came a familiar voice.

"Captain Callahan?"

The captain leaned out the window of the truck. "Hello, Sergeant Aries. Fancy meeting you out here."

By this time, his men had come out to see what the commotion was about.

"Yes, sir, I was going to say the same thing to you."

"I was just bringing these supplies to our company in Antrain. I don't know if there's any room in the back for your men, but you're welcome to hop in."

Aries peered into the cabin of the truck to see two men already sitting there. "Why did *you* have to go, sir?"

"Because some quartermasters don't listen. Check in the back, see if we have some room."

moved some boxes around and were able to squeeze six men into the truck. Aries, with his large frame, couldn't fit in the back, so he went to the front.

"Got room up here?"

"Move over, boys," ordered Callahan to the other two men, so they did.

Aries was not happy about his bulk for once, as he sat almost in the lap of one of Callahan's first sergeants.

Callahan manhandled the stick shift, between the legs of the other hapless sergeant, and got the truck moving again. "I think your company is still in Antrain, but you can stay with us until you find them."

"Thank you, sir."

The ride back had no conversation because of the noise of the truck and the bumps in the bomb-struck road. When they got to Antrain, Aries helped unload the boxes and sent his men to find somewhere to sleep. He found Callahan in his HQ, talking to his communications array. In the dim light of lanterns, Callahan looked even more romantic. He had thick legs, and a small butt from what Aries could see through the uniform. He smiled at Aries again, and Aries just wanted to scoop the man into his arms and kiss those lips.

Callahan said, "Thanks for helping out. You'd better get some rest."

"You too, Captain."

"Oh, I will. Have to finish a few things here." He turned from Aries and went back to his men.

Aries left the room without a salute and stepped outside of the house. Part of him was exhausted enough to curl up right there and sleep; another part of him wanted to go back and see where Callahan was sleeping. Unfortunately, that part kept him awake.

He found a spot in the woods. He imagined he had Callahan bent over one of the tables in that room, pounding through him like there was no tomorrow.

He used leaves to wipe up, and curled up into his bedroll, finally falling asleep.

7

"Looks like you're stuck with us, sergeant," said Callahan's XO to Aries. "We're heading west. You'll catch up with your company sooner or later."

"That's all right, I don't mind. What're my orders?"

The XO took out a map and showed it to him.

"We're taking Roumasson and heading through these hedgerows to *Trans de' Foret*." He straightened. "Think you can do that?"

"Yes, sir."

"Saddle up, then."

Aries found his men, and, joining with another squad of eight, they started heading north along the road. They met up with some German artillery, which they wiped out by going around them and attacking from the rear. Aries' blessings followed the men, and no one was injured by the time they sat down for lunch at the entrance to a large, thick forest.

"We're going to have to go in there," said the master sergeant in charge of the other men.

"I know," Aries said while they sat on the road eating their rations.

Another squad came up the road, followed by two more. They planned together. Aries listened, sometimes putting his few cents in, but, in general, the plan was sound. Just as they all got up, to get ready to go in, someone came barreling down the road. All the men moved aside for the vehicle.

It skidded to a stop in front of them. Two men — one a lieutenant by his bars — pointed back down the road they had come.

"Go back to HQ, now!"

Then, with a grinding of gears, he was off again.

Aries watched the man go. The men stood, looking at each other.

"We'll go back," said Aries. "If we're not back in an hour, then it's safe to come back."

"Right," said the master sergeant.

While the other three squads waited, Aries got his group of men going at a brisk trot back down to Antrain.

After cresting a hill, they found the company's convoy a smoking ruin. Men with stripes and bars ran around in a near panic, barking orders to other men who weren't listening. Aries sent one of his men back to the others gathered in the forest, while he took the other five among the convoy.

He found the captain's vehicle, also a smoking hulk. The remains of two men lay in it, burned beyond recognition, their bones exposed, flesh blackened. A pit formed in his stomach.

"Where's the captain?" yelled Aries. But no one was listening.

He looked at the two bodies in the Jeep and approached them, ignoring the sweet smell of burnt flesh. One of the bodies was tall - the XO. The other was of medium height, but not built like Callahan.

He grabbed a corporal with a bloody face as he wandered in Aries' direction.

"Where's Callahan?"

"They came ... he, I don't know."

Aries almost threw the man aside.

His men kept walking north and bumped into another convoy that had stopped on the road because of the mess this one was in. It was Company D of the 116th, and their captain was swearing up a storm to get a bulldozer to clear the mess out of the way.

Aries checked the other vehicles. He went back to Callahan's jeep and looked around. The side of the road had been churned up by many people running. He saw paths through the fields of men pushing down the grain as they scattered.

"Where are you?" he whispered, looking at the paths of grain.

Unfortunately, tracking was not one of the blessings of his Lady. He glanced around to make sure nobody was following, and then headed out into the field.

He still could hear the commotion behind him as he went deeper into the field. Aries found one GI lying face down in a trampled section of grain. Ignoring that foreboding sight, he headed further in, following a different trail. This one led to the woods.

Aries growled in frustration. His gut instincts said to go into the woods, but his head was saying that he needed to report in, to check and see if Callahan was indeed missing.

His gut never steered him wrong.

8

He came out to a clearing. He pulled out his compass, and then noticed a drop on it. Then felt some drops hit his face when he looked up.

"Aw, dammit," he moaned, and checked his bearings. Aries headed southwest, away from the division, going further south than he had intended. Since Aries had no map, every field looked like every other field.

He stood on tiptoes to see if he could see any more flattened grain. The chances of that were going to be slim. He knew he was lost.

The rain fell harder.

He walked along the tree line, still heading generally southwest. Aries glanced ahead to see if there were any flat patches of grain, and kept walking. His watch said it was 1730.

Normally, that was dinner, but now Aries wasn't sure where the company was at all. He wanted to go back northwest, to run into his own men, but his gut kept saying to go this way.

So he went. As luck would have it, he found a spot where the grain was trampled near the tree line.

With an upward glance, Aries whispered, "Thank you, Lady," in his old native tongue.

Aries followed the path. Although the sky was gray and raining, it was still daytime. He could see there had been a lot of people walking; it looked like four abreast.

He followed the trail, coming up onto a rise, and saw a house. He also saw trucks and other vehicles, so he kept low and crept closer. It was as he feared: someone opened a door to a truck and he saw a swastika painted on its side.

"Shit," he hissed, and ran the rest of the way toward the barn, still crouched.

He reached the closest barn and threw himself against it, staying beneath the window. Still keeping low, he crept around the building and pushed the door in. A pair of horses gazed at him and snorted in surprise.

"Sorry," he muttered, and crept back, going to the next building.

He heard a couple of squawks, which meant this was the hen house. He peered over the windowsill: he counted two chickens and a rooster. Ducking back down, Aries ducked to the left. Another shed was there, so he used that for cover. He moved closer to the trucks and the house.

Soon, Aries found himself behind a garage. He distinctly heard the Germans speaking.

"I wonder where Patton is."

"The Colonel said he isn't here."

The Germans started to walk, crunching along the area between the house and the garage. If they passed the garage, and looked to their right, they would see him there. He waited, his rifle at his hip.

"I wouldn't mind going a few rounds with him. It's better than all this running."

"Fred! Kris! We're going to take the prisoners now."

Aries peered around the corner to see the two Germans standing with their backs to him, and another man further back, standing near a truck.

"Shit," Aries whispered, and jerked back.

The stable was far away, but he had to run for it. He heard the truck start up. Rising, he bolted across the field, in plain sight to anyone who might be looking in his direction, and dove into the stable.

Leaving his rifle by the door, he unlocked one of the stalls, grabbing a bridle. "Going to ride you bareback, sweetheart," he said in French. "So please forgive me."

Aries fit the bridle onto the horse, leading her out of the stable. He swung himself onto the horse's back. Tugging on the bridle to lead her out into the field near the trees, he saw a truck travelling to his left on the road. Aries jerked the reins to the left, turning the horse toward the direction of the truck.

The horse took the lead and started galloping as he pressed his legs tightly around her shoulders. Aries stayed low. As the truck stopped at an intersection at the end of the hedgerows, Aries jumped the hedges about a half kilometer away. The rain-slicked asphalt made the horse slip, and Aries almost lost his balance, but regained it and the horse's.

"Atta girl!" he yelled, and got her back on the road.

The truck took a left and he followed it. Head level with the horse's, he listened to her pant as he dug his legs in and she ran. She was probably not going to catch up, but Aries would at least have a good lead. The truck slowed down, and eased to the left to avoid a bomb crater, but he didn't stop. Aries almost caught up to the truck before it cleared the crater and started to pick up speed again. He jumped over the crater and was nearly level with the truck.

He looked at the truck to see if there was any way to grab a handhold, then saw a man's face in the mirror ahead of him. The man leaned out with a pistol and fired at Aries.

Aries slowed down and got behind the truck. The horse was starting to wheeze. Aries knew that had to jump for it.

Just then, the back flap opened. A German with a rifle stood up, taking aim at Aries.

The truck hit a bump. The German fell backwards into the truck, the shot going up and through the canvas top. With one more squeeze of his legs and a push forward, Aries got close enough to the truck that he could leap into it if he tried.

Instead, the truck slammed on its brakes, and Aries and the horse barreled right into the truck. The horse hit her chest on the tailgate, while Aries was dumped inside. He slammed into the back of the cab of the truck, but wasn't dazed. Righting himself, he now faced two men with their pistols pointed right at him.

The truck had stopped, and someone opened the cab door. Aries looked around and saw that one of the men in the truck was Callahan. His left thigh was bandaged; blood seeped through it.

"Aries?" he said, surprised.

Aries nodded. He slowly got to his feet, his head bowed, but his eyes on the two men with pistols. A shot from outside made him jump: someone had just killed the horse. A Kraut lifted the flap and Aries saw the dead horse on the road. He whispered a prayer for its soul to run free.

The German outside yelled at him in German. "Hands up!"

Aries made like he didn't understand, and took two steps forward. The men with the guns waved them at him threateningly. Aries put his hands up and sat down on the bench, across from Callahan.

"Tie him up," said the man outside.

"We have no rope, sir."

The outside German threw up his hands and turned from them, walking back to the front of the truck. It started up again.

Callahan stared at Aries. "What the hell was that stunt?"

"Was trying to save you," he said, looking sheepishly at the dozen or so men and not again at Callahan.

"You could have gotten yourself killed!"

"I knew what I was doing."

"You did, so now you got yourself captured."

He glanced at the two men. "Not for long."

"What's that supposed to mean?"

He looked at Callahan and grinned. "Hold onto your seats. It's going to be a bumpy ride."

Aries put his hands under his seat. Callahan saw it, and copied the movement. The rest of the men did too.

Aries suddenly got up and, swaying with the motion of the vehicle, leapt at the German soldier diagonally opposite him at the tail edge of the truck. The other German across from him shouted and unloaded his pistol on him. Aries punched the first German hard enough to daze him, relieved him of his weapon, and then shot the other German, who fell back against the canvas of the truck.

Aries tossed the first German over the tailgate. Although he could take injury, it didn't mean it didn't hurt. He felt the bullets worm their way back out. One of them hit the floor, bouncing.

The men stared at him; one of them made the sign of the cross. Aries grunted and, with a glance at Callahan, went over to the window between the cab and the back. Holding the gun by the butt, to keep his hand stronger, Aries punched through the glass of the cab. He fed the pistol through the shattered window and shot right, then left.

He pulled his hand out just as the truck drifted left, hit the side of the road, and rolled sideways. The men on the passenger side of the truck fell onto the men on the driver's side; one man fell out of the back.

Aries got up first, checking Callahan. Callahan had his hands tied behind his back, and one of the other guys was trying to get off of him, but dug his elbow into Callahan's thigh.

Callahan grunted, while Aries got the guy off of him. All of the men started jumping out, rolling onto the grass at the side of the road. One man had gotten untied, and was untying the rest.

Aries untied Callahan. "We got everybody?"

"I think so," Callahan said, getting up on his good leg. He tried to put weight on his bad one, but it didn't hold.

"I got him!" Aries yelled. "You guys, get the hell outta here!"

He obviously didn't have to say it twice, because when he looked around in the rain, nobody was there.

He turned to Callahan and got on his left side. "Lean on me."

Callahan sighed. "Aries, you might as well leave me. I'm injured and —"

"I'm not leaving you, sir," Aries said firmly. "We have to find some shelter."

"You're stubborn, you know that?" said Callahan.

He turned around for Callahan and squatted slightly. "Climb on."

Callahan sighed, and put his arms around Aries' broad shoulders. Aries took the hands, crossed them in front of his chest, and then stood up, lifting Callahan off the ground. He left the truck, heading away from the west and into the woods.

9

Aries had been given the blessing of endurance, though he knew he was going to crash hard when he stopped. He kept heading northeast, hoping he would run into someone.

They were crossing a pasture when Callahan said, "Aries, stop."

Aries did, lowering Callahan slowly to the ground. Callahan was pale, and his bandage was soaked. "You must be ... tired."

"I think I see a village up ahead," he lied. "Just a little more."

"Let me rest here."

"No, sir." Aries pulled him up, knowing what those words usually foretold. They usually meant he was going to dig a grave where they lay down. Callahan moaned, and let Aries pick him up, still in a fireman's carry. "C'mon, not too much farther to go."

They didn't find a village, but they did find a farm. He ran toward it as the rain got worse. Heading to the barn, he found it padlocked. Hoping that Callahan didn't see, he grabbed the lock and twisted it open.

Aries pulled open the door and shut it behind them. He smelled the fresh clean hay of the barn, and the aroma of animals. Turning, he came face to face with a cow, who mooed at him.

"Right," he said, and walked around the cow to a spot toward the back of the barn. He lay Callahan down again at the base of a bunch of hay.

"Captain. Callahan. Bill!"

He opened his eyes and focused them on Aries. "Aries. Where are we?"

"A barn," he said. There was a lantern. He debated whether to use it.

Callahan sat up against the pile of hay. "At least it's dry." He lifted his injured leg, looking at the bloody bandages. "They didn't even stitch it."

"What happened?"

"They shot me while I was getting out of the truck."

"You weren't in your jeep?"

"I never ride in that jeep." He nodded upwards. "Have any food?"

"No, sir."

"Forget the 'sirs', Aries. Right now it's just you and me, and we're stuck here."

"All right then. I'm going to go check the big house, see if —"

The door to the barn opened and Aries turned, the German pistol in his hand. A boy whistled as he walked down the small aisle near the cow, and then stopped short upon seeing the men in the dim light.

He dropped the pail he was carrying with a clang and ran back out.

"Shit," Aries spat.

"Language," said Callahan.

"Do you know French?"

"Only from school."

Aries sighed. "I'll do the talking."

"Aries," said Callahan with a wisp of awe. "Who are you? Superman?"

"No," he replied, standing up and next to Callahan. "Not quite."

The door opened again, and this time a lantern lit the room.

Both men squinted. A voice called from the door.

"*Parlez-vous français?*"

"*Oui*," said Aries.

The man continued in French, "Who are you?"

"Americans. Who are you?"

"Oh, thank God." The man stepped inside, leaning an antiquated rifle against the door. "You don't know how long we've been praying for this to happen!"

The man was tall, thin and gaunt, and ran toward the two Americans. He hugged and kissed Aries on both cheeks, and held him at arm's length, as if he was a long-lost brother. He looked down at Callahan.

"You're hurt."

"He doesn't speak French."

Callahan was trying to get up and Aries went to his side to help him.

"Do you have a doctor?"

"There's a doctor in the village. But there are Germans there."

"Great," Aries said in English, and told Callahan what the man said.

Callahan said, "See if he can give us some food, and tell him we'll leave so that he doesn't get in trouble."

When Aries told the man, he shook his head. After a rapid fire of French, the man smiled, waiting for a reply.

"He said that he'll get us food and a doctor tomorrow. He wants to show us something."

"I don't know, do you trust him?"

"Not particularly."

"I'll go see."

"No, I will."

Callahan gave him a look. "Don't make me pull rank on you."

"I thought you said to forget it."

"Fine, we'll both go."

Aries said something to the man, who nodded, bobbing his head. He started for the ladder to the loft.

Callahan looked up, then back at Aries. "Maybe you'd better go."

Aries grinned, and left Callahan near a pillar. Aries climbed the ladder. The Frenchman lifted a few bales of hay, setting them aside, and then made a presentation.

"He's got a two-way radio up here," Aries said. "The antenna's inside and I guess he puts it outside to pick up signals."

"Think we can get a hold of the 116th?"

"I don't even know where we are." Aries made a downward motion with his hand, and the man put the bales of hay back while he climbed down. "I can't give a report if I don't know where we are."

"Ask him."

Aries did.

"*Nouvoitou.*"

Callahan shrugged. "No idea where that is in relation to where we were."

"I didn't memorize the map, either."

Aries started to sway. The adrenaline was crashing. He was going to pass out. Callahan reached a hand out and grabbed Aries, though if Aries fell, Callahan would fall right on top of him.

"Food," Callahan said, and mimed eating something.

"*Oui!*" the man said, and snapped something at the boy who had come in with the pail. Aries stepped forward, barely keeping his feet.

Callahan limped back to his place at the base of the pile of hay, and Aries followed. He finally collapsed, sitting down hard.

"We'll get some food into you, Aries."

"Too tired to eat," Aries said.

"Sleep then, I'll watch over you."

Aries smiled, and closed his eyes. "It's supposed to be the other way around," he muttered, as he drifted off to sleep.

IO

Aries woke up instantly, his eyes snapping open. He took in his surroundings. A barn. Hay. Callahan asleep with his back to him. Aries studied his sleeping form. Callahan had taken off his jacket and used it as a pillow, so he was clad only in the Army issued A-shirt. He'd taken off his belt and boots as well. Aries's eyes studied the contour of the man: how nice and perfect.

Aries crotch hurt with desire and other needs, so he tried to be quiet and roll away from Callahan. The swish of the hay made Callahan stir. He rolled onto his back and opened his eyes, looking at Aries. He smiled, his eyes crinkling again. Aries couldn't help but smile back.

"You snore," Callahan said, yawning and stretching.

"Sorry," Aries said, and got up, also stretching. "What happened after I went to sleep?"

"We got some food, and I used my high school French to thank him. His name is Jacques."

"Any left?"

Callahan looked around. "There was some, but they probably took it away. Mice, you know. Just some bread and soft cheese." He yawned and sat up, stretching again. He tried to get up, but Aries was already at his side, helping him. "You get shot at, point blank, and live. You know French. And you're my crutch?"

"I don't mind, Bill."

He chuckled, "That's the first time you've not called me 'sir'."

"Like you said - "

"Yeah, yeah, I know. Let's go find an outhouse."

It wasn't very far from the barn. Callahan went first, and then Aries, who had finally calmed down enough to piss. He heard voices and stepped out to see Callahan trying to talk to Jacques. Standing outside of the house along with Jacques was his wife, who was smiling and happy to see him. She saw Aries and waved, coming over to him.

"We are so glad you are here, sir," she said, and kissed him on both cheeks. "If you are here, then the rest of the Americans are not far behind?"

"I hope not," he replied, as the woman guided him back to the two men.

Callahan looked helplessly at Aries. "I think I heard the word 'medicine' in what he was saying."

Aries spoke to Jacques and translated to Callahan, "He said he's going to try to get the doctor away today. If not the doctor, then the veterinarian."

Callahan raised an eyebrow. "A vet?"

"It's more plausible for the vet to come here since he has animals. And sometimes the Germans go with the doctor to see who he's seeing." Jacques spoke some more. "In the meantime, he'll make a crutch for you."

"He doesn't have to do that —"

"He said he's been making too many coffins, it would be a pleasant change."

Callahan turned to Jacques, "*Merci beaucoup.*"

"It's nothing," translated Aries.

"We'd better go back to the barn."

They spoke some more, then Aries led Callahan back to the barn. "He'll bring us some breakfast."

"I know what trouble he could get into by having us here," Callahan said. "At least we have the barn."

Jacques came with them into the barn, his wife following with a tray of food. Jacques measured Callahan for his crutch. Aries was able to hollow out a place in the hay for the two to stay in if the Germans came.

After breakfast, Aries helped Jacques hitch his horse to a wagon. A cotton canvas covered something in the back. Aries lifted the canvas to see two caskets, one large, one small. He frowned as he set the canvas down and smoothed it over the cargo.

The boy milked the cow, keeping an eye on Callahan. Aries watched the boy and tried to hold a conversation with him, but the boy would answer him curtly.

A short time later, the wife arrived with a basket of rags and clothes. Everything was clean, and Aries took the rags, putting them aside.

"You're going to have to get out of those pants, Bill," Aries said. "I have to change that bandage."

"If you take it off, it's going to bleed again."

Aries frowned. He was right. Unless someone sewed the wound shut, it would bleed profusely again.

"Let's see if these clothes fit, at least."

Callahan struggled out of the pants. Aries almost bent to help him, but didn't know how Callahan would have taken it.

Finally, he saw that Callahan had a hard time lifting his body and pulling up the pants. "Let me help you."

Callahan sat, panting, as Aries put his hands on Callahan's waist. That electric touch made them look into each other's eyes.

Both men moved at the same time, leaning their heads forward to meet in a tentative kiss. Then Aries cupped the back of Callahan's head and kissed him passionately, holding his head still, opening himself up to Callahan. Callahan took it and, with a groan Aries, deepened the kiss. His dreams were coming true.

They broke, looking at each other again, panting. They kissed again. Aries gently pushed Callahan down into the hay as one hand started feeling up Callahan's chest. Callahan awkwardly put his arms around Aries, his hands caressing Aries' back.

When Aries came up for air, Callahan whispered, "Not right now."

Aries kissed Callahan's cheek and jaw. "It won't take long."

He took Callahan's hand and brought it to his crotch, swollen and hard. Callahan moaned as Aries kissed his neck, and then his hand gripped Callahan's crotch, which was also hard.

"No, no, it won't," Callahan said, pushing the underwear down to his knees.

Aries fished out his manhood for him, and Callahan sighed. Aries bent his head down and took it in his mouth, while unbuttoning his pants and getting himself out. Callahan sighed and *ahhe*d, and lay back, his eyes closed.

Aries knew exactly what he was doing, and got his rocks off faster than Callahan did. When Callahan came, Aries swallowed it, enjoying the salty-musky taste of him. Part of his dream had come true. As he lifted his head, he hoped that the other part would come true as well.

"Oh ..." panted Callahan, as Aries tucked himself away, and then buttoned up his pants.

Aries moved the hay around to cover up the evidence of his sated desire. Callahan opened his eyes slowly and gazed at Aries.

"That was - I don't know what that was."

"Did you like it?"

Callahan gave him a lopsided grin, "Oh, yes."

"Then it was good."

"Hm, yes."

Aries lay next to Callahan, wanting to pull him into his arms, but not sure how he would take it if he did.

Callahan stared at the ceiling. "I think I'll have to go to confession after all this is over."

"You're Catholic?"

He nodded. "Born and raised. I know, huh?" He reached over and touched Aries's face. "Can you do that again sometime? I'm in for a penny, so ..."

Aries laughed, turned his head and kissed Callahan's palm. "For a moment there, I thought you were going to say, 'We can't do this anymore, Aries'."

"Are you kidding? If I knew these feelings I had for you was all right with you, I wouldn't have been so guilt-ridden over these last few weeks."

"Your God will be upset."

"My God? You're not Catholic? Or Christian, even?"

"No. I come from a different time and place."

Callahan turned sideways to look at Aries. "Tell me."

Aries wanted so badly to tell him. So, he did.

"I'm originally from Eire. You know it as Ireland."

"Well, I could tell you were Irish."

"I died in Bosnia."

"You died?"

Aries nodded, his hand now on Callahan's arm. Callahan brought his hand away. "You're - resurrected?"

"Not by Jesus. A goddess came to the underworld and brought me to this Earth to help and protect humanity."

"A goddess?"

"Ishtar. Babylonian goddess of Love and War."

"So that's why you took all those bullets."

He nodded. "We all can."

"We?"

"There's others like me. Brothers in the *Mul'apin* — The Zodiac."

Callahan looked into Aries's eyes. "You're not kidding."

He entwined his fingers with Callahan's. "I'm not kidding."

"Which one are you?"

"*Ku'Mal*. Aries, the Ram."

Callahan laughed. "Head down and going forward, that's you, all right!"

Aries chuckled, "That's me."

Callahan pulled his hand out from Aries' and touched his shirt instead.

"Why are you telling me all this?" he said very quietly.

"Because —"

The door to the barn opened. Both men rolled away from each other as Jacques entered, the doctor in tow. He carried a black bag, and straightened his glasses as he entered. Aries stood up.

"Good evening," the doctor said in English. "What do we have here?"

"I got shot," said Callahan.

"Please let me see the wound?"

Callahan glanced up at Aries, and then undid his pants. He pushed them down, pulling his shirt down to cover his groin. The new bandage had a small blood spot on it.

"It is clotting," said the doctor. "That is good."

He undid the bandages, and looked at the wound.

Aries couldn't smell it, so it wasn't infected.

The doctor examined the wound and then reached into his black bag. He took some tweezers, and stuck them into the hole. Aries winced, and Callahan's body tensed, while he gasped in pain.

The doctor shook his head, pulling the bloody tweezers out.

"I cannot take it out. I suggest closing the wound and going to another surgeon later."

Callahan panted, sweating. "All right, Doc."

The doctor took out some twine and a needle. He threaded the needle.

Aries said, "Put a flame to that tip, doc. Shit, even I know that."

"I do not have matches."

Aries took down the box of matches above the lantern near them. He handed the box to the doctor, who glared at Aries. He used the bottom of Callahan's shoe to start the match, and stuck the tip into the flame.

Callahan gritted his teeth as the doctor sewed up the wound, and then wrapped it up again loosely.

"It should stop bleeding in the next day or so," said the doctor. "Keep it clean and if it smells bad, call me again."

Callahan let out a breath he was holding. "Right," he grunted.

Jacques thanked the doctor profusely and helped him get up and out. Aries kept his eye on him as he left.

"I don't trust him," Callahan said.

"Me neither." He lit the lantern as Jacques came back in. "I don't trust that doctor."

Jacques said, "He won't say anything."

"Why?"

"If he does, the town will tell them he's Jewish, and he knows it."

"Is he?"

"He was a recent convert before the Nazis came. His wife and children left him because of it."

Aries took a breath and let it out slowly. There was a knock on the door.

"Jacques?" came his wife's voice.

"In here," he said.

The man came inside and shut the door behind him.

"Here you are. How's Cecilia?" He patted the head of the cow. He tipped his hat to Callahan. "*Bonsoir, monsieur.* Robert Collett."

"Bill," said Callahan, nodding once.

"And John?" said Collett, motioning to Aries.

"Yes," said Callahan. "Or *oui*."

"My English ... is as good as *Deutsche*."

"Better than my French."

Collett let off some rapid-fire sentences, as Aries translated.

"He's a contact from the Free French Militia, and he has contacts with the RAF but not the Army yet, though it's expected that they'll be in the area within the next few days, since Patton is driving through France, according to last night's radio reports."

"We can hunker down for a few days," said Callahan.

"That's up to our host," said Aries, looking at Jacques.

Aries asked Jacques if he would allow them to stay the few days until the Allies got to them. Jacques glanced at Collett.

Collett shook his head saying, "*Non*," a couple of times firmly. "I can't - they are watching me."

"Which means you could have brought them here!" Jacques said hotly.

Collett went to the door and opened it. When he did, three German soldiers in black uniforms ran in, followed by another one in an officer's cap. Aries saw their markings: two lightning flashes on the collar. SS.

Callahan groaned and looked up at the ceiling.

Aries said in fast and furious French, "You said I could trust him!"

Jacques said in a voice that could make ice, "I thought I could." Then he spat at Collett.

"I'm sorry," said Collett, looking down.

"You traitor!"

Meanwhile, one soldier had grabbed Callahan, kicking away his crutch. Callahan leaned heavily on the soldier. Aries was held by two soldiers. The German SS officer walked up to Aries and punched him in the stomach.

Aries doubled over, exhaling, as expected, but it didn't do what it was supposed to do. Aries had been punched there numerous times and had built up a tolerance over the years. He could come back fighting if he wanted to. But now was not the time.

Then the German walked up to Callahan. "And you, you're new."

"William Callahan, Sergeant," said Callahan.

Aries blinked. *Why did he bump himself down a few ranks?*

Callahan got punched in the stomach, too. He bent in half, his weight going on his bad leg, and he almost fell.

"Tie them up," the man in the fancier black uniform ordered. One of the soldiers released Aries to get some rope.

Callahan stood up straight finally. The soldier threw him against the main pillar and tied him there. He did the same to Aries, tying him back-to-back with Callahan. Aries made fists to make it harder for them to tie the ropes.

Aries saw Jacques slug Collette.

As the two men started to fight in the barn, two of the soldiers rushed in to break it up. One knocked over the lantern and the book of matches. The kerosene leaked from the lantern, leaving a line of fire that led to the matches, which ignited immediately.

"Time to go," said the SS officer.

Aries tugged at the rope - it was loose. He watched as they left.

The hay that they had slept in went up next. The cow mooed mournfully.

Aries tugged again at the rope, noticing that Callahan was doing the same. His left hand came free. He untangled it from the ropes, then undid his right hand.

"They'll be outside the door, Aries," said Callahan, as Aries started to undo his knots.

"We're not going out the door."

The knots were all tangled, and it took Aries a bit to get them undone. By then, the loft was going up.

"If we don't get out —"

"We're going to get out."

He finished untying Callahan. He stood up, still leaning on his right leg, but better balanced.

"How?"

Aries grinned and said, "I'm a fire sign."

He picked Callahan up in a bridal carry and started to walk into the flames.

Callahan buried his head in Aries's shoulder and curled up tight against him as Aries walked through the flames to an open breach on the opposite side. They heard the cracking of the wood above them, the roar of flames around them. Aries got through the hole and, as he did, the loft came crashing down, throwing sparks and cinders that didn't even touch the two men.

Then Aries broke out into a run across the field as the barn went up in flames.

Callahan lifted his head and said, "What about the cow?"

"Fuck the cow," Aries yelled, and kept running.

II

It was full night when Aries tripped and fell, rolling onto the grass. He dropped Callahan, who went flying out of his arms, about three feet away from him.

"Ow," was all Callahan said.

Aries, panting, turned over and looked at the night sky. He couldn't run anymore. He was exhausted.

Callahan crawled through the grass over to him. "Aries, Aries! Are you alright?"

"Catching — my breath —"

Callahan sighed in relief and lay his head on Aries's chest. Aries automatically put his hand on Callahan's head.

"You ran for hours."

"I don't know," Aries could only say.

He suspected he ran for a long time, past dusk, into the dark where he could still see in it — jumping over hedgerows, avoiding farms and lights. Caressing Callahan's brown hair, he stared up at the sky. He could pick out the constellation of Leo, Virgo, the Seven Sisters, and the Ursae.

"How old are you? Callahan suddenly asked.

"I stopped counting after 500."

"You have a few years on me, then."

Aries chuckled, "Just a few."

Callahan lifted his head. "You never told me why you told me all that, before."

Aries stroked Callahan's face. "Because I want to spend the rest of my life with you."

Callahan jerked back, startled.

Aries looked away. "I'm sorry," Aries said.

Callahan shook his head, as if to clear it. "But you live a long life."

"Not if I find someone I want to spend it with."

"What about your goddess?"

"She's the goddess of War and Love. She understands."

"So I'll live as long as you?"

"No. I'll live as long as *you*."

Callahan said, "I wouldn't want you to die the same day I do."

Aries shrugged and brought his hand up again to Callahan's face. "And when we die, we're joined forever and put among the stars." He pointed upward.

"You believe that?"

"I know it."

Callahan turned to his side and rolled onto his back, looking up at the stars. "Beautiful."

Aries found Callahan's hand and took it, squeezing. "Yes."

"Have you ever been in love, Aries?"

"Just this once. Right now."

Callahan squeezed Aries' hand. "Me too."

They lay there looking up at the sky, even while the planes sailed overhead, a thrumming roar, and could hear a distant siren wailing, and the distant booms of bombs hitting the earth.

Aries didn't notice he'd had fallen asleep until he felt the heat creep up on him. Callahan had curled up beside him, laying on his chest. Aries woke up like he normally did, and bent his head to kiss Callahan's hair.

"Wake up, sunshine."

"Uhhh ... I fell asleep?"

Callahan stretched his arms out sideways, and saw that he was on Aries's chest. Callahan scrambled up.

"Why such a rush?"

"Well, one, I have to water the garden, and two, I didn't know how you would feel about that."

"Bill. I come from a time and place where men having sex with each other is not unusual."

"That long ago?"

"The time of the Romans, when they still ruled Gaul."

"You're going to have to tell me more details sometime," he said, and struggled up.

He limped a few yards away and pissed in the grass. Aries did the same.

"Now, where are we?"

"Your guess is as good as mine."

"Well, east is that way," he faced the rising sun. "North must be that way," he pointed to his left.

"Let's head that way."

They walked through pastureland, and then through farmland, where corn rotted on the stalk. Aries took some of the corn off the cob and ate it straight. Callahan did the same at Aries' direction.

"This tastes like - raw dough."

"It's pure starch," Aries said. "Gives you energy." He sucked on the cob, drawing the juices from it.

They came upon another farm.

"What do you think?" asked Aries.

"I think we should avoid them. Any way we can follow a road?"

"Have to find one first," he said.

They followed one of the stone walls that marked off farming fields from fallow. That led to a cow path, which they followed.

Aries suddenly stopped. "Do you hear that?"

Callahan stopped, listening.

"Vehicles," he said.

"We're getting near a road."

They kept walking down the cow path, until a fence blocked their way. Beyond the fence was a road. They jumped the fence, with Aries helping Callahan over it. Following the road, Aries stopped and listened.

Callahan heard it, too. "What if they're Jerries?"

"I carry you away again," said Aries.

The vehicles began getting closer; they could hear their roar. As they crested a small hill, they could see the leading vehicle of the convoy. It had a star on its hood.

"Thank God," said Callahan, his whole body sagging in relief.

"Let's sit down over here until they get here." He pointed to a trench on the side of the road, and both of them ducked down into it.

The first vehicle saw them and stopped; both men had their hands up.

"Are we glad to see you," said Callahan.

"What's your name?" yelled the corporal, a little too loud.

"Captain William Callahan, and this is Sergeant John Aries, from the 29th infantry."

"29th? You're a long way from home," said the driver with a Midwestern accent.

"You're from the 8th."

"What's going on, private?" came someone from another vehicle.

"These two men say they're from the 29th."

Aries helped Callahan out of the trench.

"Lieutenant," said Callahan. "We'd like to report to your superior officer."

"Private, escort these two men, please."

Aries knew they were going to be not trusted until they were verified, so he went along with Callahan. Callahan walked side by side with Aries as the private held the gun to them. They arrived at a jeep, where a man was standing up.

"What the hell is going on?"

"Found these two men, sir," said the lieutenant. "They're from the 29th."

"No shit. Who's your CO?"

"Colonel Philip Dwyer, Captain."

"Your name?"

"Captain William Callahan and Sergeant John Aries."

"Ain't you a little too east for being the 29th?"

"To tell you the truth, Captain, we don't know where we are."

"We just liberated Rennes, if that helps. No? You won't mind if we wait a little while we check your bona fides, do you?"

"Not at all," said Callahan. "Though could we have something to drink?"

"Get them some water," yelled the captain. "And radio HQ, tell them we have two guys here from the 29th."

They served the captain first, but he gave the cup to Aries. Aries took it, drank it down and gave it back.

"It's gonna take a while," said the captain. Then the radio squawked.

"Blue Bonnet, those two men are MIA, repeat, MIA."

"Lemme see your tags."

Both men leaned forward and showed him their dog tags.

"Tell them they're not missing any more. You're injured, there, son?" he said to Callahan.

"Yes. Fractured thigh."

"Get him to the rear and bring him back to Rennes."

"Excuse me," said Callahan, "I'm not leaving without Sergeant Aries." He said, seriously and straight, "He saved my life numerous times."

Aries crossed his arms, as if daring anyone to make him move.

"Go with him," said the captain.

12

Promoted again, Lieutenant Aries became an adjutant to Major Callahan. Wounded with a purple heart, Callahan refused to return home. So he spent the duration of the war in the rear, limping his way through, until the liberation of Berlin, when he and Lieutenant Aries finally were discharged at the same time.

LEO

♌

BOISE, IDAHO
SEPTEMBER 8, 1935

I

I WATCHED THE TRAIN PULL INTO THE STATION. We had three wagons ready to haul the gear necessary for the stage production of *The Wonderful Wizard of Oz*. This train contained the original cast members from the New York production.

What the hell caused them to come all the way to Boise, I had no idea.

Not to mention, the entire production would be weirdly out of place in the Fox Theatre, which had Egyptian themes throughout. It was supposed to look like King Tut's tomb.

"Jack," the supervisor called to me. "C'mon."

I was the strongest person in the group, and the one with the most endurance, so they usually had me do the heavy work. The sets, colored beautifully and cheerfully for this drab town, were cut into multiple pieces, but were huge and heavy.

I had to take off my shirt at one point, as did a few of the other stage hands. I sweated under the beating sun, but it gave me more strength, not sapped it, like it did with the other guys.

As I laid up one of the scenes onto the wagon, I turned to see someone staring at me. Staring. Like an awestruck staring.

He was short, with very short dark hair. Clean shaven. Younger than me — but then, everyone in town was younger than me, even "Old Man" Hoggis. I beat everyone by a good hundred years or so. But I looked in my thirties. So when I say he's younger? He's in his twenties.

I stopped and stared back at him. I smiled and waved. He waved back.

"Jack!" someone screamed, as a wooden scene started to fall out of his hands.

I rushed to the side and caught it before it fell and possibly broke. "I got this."

"Man, how can you do this?"

I grinned at him. "Magic, my friend."

"Magic, my ass."

"Maybe that too."

Joey howled with laughter. He knew. A few of the stagehands knew that I liked the actors, even though the actresses liked me more. As long as I did my work, didn't complain, and didn't come on to the workers that didn't know, I was safe in my job.

Now the actors ... that's a whole other story.

2

We hauled the wagons back to the Fox Theatre in downtown. There were cars and people and all sorts of traffic in the way. The theater was on a corner, but we had to go through the back and unload in complete secrecy.

Not quite complete. Some kids always seemed to hang around outside the back of the theater. All of them, if they ever went to the theater at all, would end up in the peanut gallery. Going to the theater was not on the top of their parents' lists of things to do on a Saturday night.

"Whatcha unloadin'?" they'd usually ask.

We made it a point to never tell them what it was for. Let them find out on the marquee.

They loved to watch us, and try to figure out what the bits of scenes were for. They especially liked to watch me, to see if I would buckle under the weight of a scene if I carried it myself. I never did.

The actors showed up, having been brought by car from the railroad. We had to wait for them to get into the building, although sometimes they stood around and watched us. This time was no exception, really.

The man who watched me before stayed outside to watch us again. I flexed and lifted one of the heavier scenes and carried it in by myself.

That was a little much for me, though, and I had to take a breather. I went back outside and walked up to him, still shirtless, sweaty, and breathing heavy. I wanted a cold beer, but I'd settle for five minutes of sitting down.

"Hey," I said to the man.

He nodded to me. "You're the strong man of the group, aren't you?"

I laughed. "How did you guess?"

"You're impressing the kids."

"They don't need the impressing."

"Mmmhmm." He looked me up and down, and I knew he was like me.

That wasn't uncommon with most of the actors. The handsome actors from New York were almost always attracted to me, and we would often end up upstairs in one of the closets.

I wiped my sweaty palm against my pants and held out my hand.

"Jack Leonard."

"Artie Hill," he said, shaking my hand.

"Are you an actor?"

"I play the Cowardly Lion."

I almost burst out laughing. "You don't seem very cowardly."

"It's all an act. All of it."

"Even you talking to me?"

He exhaled slowly. Before I could ask him anything else, someone called my name.

"See you," I called, and walked back to the wagon with the scenery on it.

When I looked back, he was gone.

3

After putting the scenery in order of display in the back of the theater, we were finally set loose. All of us stagehands went to the speakeasy — a legal bar now, but old habits die hard — across the street. Seven hot, big, sweaty men crowded into the small bar and we demanded the coldest beer they had.

They got the bottles closest to the ice and gave us six. Little Joey was a teetotaler, and asked for cold coffee instead. That settled everyone down.

I was on my third beer when Artie strolled in with three other men dressed in fancy clothes. One of them turned his nose up at us and walked back out.

Fuck him, I thought.

Artie came right up to me.

"I'll buy everyone a round," he said to the bartender behind me.

All seven of us *hurrah*ed. I switched to whiskey, since he was buying.

"All settled in, Artie?" I asked him.

"I haven't been to the hotel yet. But you guys did well with handling the scenery. I've seen some other men not give a care about it."

"I've been doing this for years." I waved my bottle to the men. "Most of these guys know better."

Artie nodded. He requested a bourbon on the rocks from the bartender. I knocked back my whiskey and winced. Not the best, but it would do in this town.

"Want another one?" Artie said, pointing to the empty shot glass.

"Nah, I still have to walk home tonight."

"Stumble. Bartender, give the man another one."

It took a lot to get me drunk, but I acted that way after the eighth shot, leaning hard against the bar. Obviously, Artie wanted me drunk.

He grinned at me. "I think I'd better cut you off," he said.

"Whatever gives you tha' 'deah."

"C'mon, Jack," he said.

The other men had already gone home to their wives and girls. Artie put my arm around his shoulders and almost toppled over from my weight when I leaned into him.

"I got you," Artie said, standing straight and guiding me out of the bar.

He brought me to the hotel instead of my apartment. I knew what he wanted. He guided me to the elevator, and that's where I "sobered up" .

"Where are you taking me?" I asked, already knowing.

"My room, so you can sleep it off."

"Uh huh," I said, and he got off on the third floor. I still had my arm around his shoulders, more for comfort than need.

He fumbled for his key in his pocket, and calmly unlocked the door. He'd obviously done this enough times. But then, so had I.

As soon as he opened the door, I was on him. I kissed him, entwining his tongue with mine, pushed him inside.

He backed up, trying to get out of my embrace. I kicked the door closed.

He finally pulled his head back. "Wait," he said.

"This is what you want, isn't it?" I said, grinning at him.

"Let me lock the door."

He squeezed past me to the door and pushed in the bolt. As soon as he did that, I grabbed him by the waist and yanked him inside.

"Wait!"

But I wasn't about to, and dragged him backwards to the bed. I fell back on it, taking him with me. I untucked his shirt and thrust my hands beneath it to cup his chest He was thin, kind of bony — not my usual type.

He gave up struggling, which disappointed me. He unbuttoned his shirt and let it flop to the sides while I groped his chest. Then my hands went down to his waist, shoved past his belt and into his pants.

He gasped, sat up, and jumped off me. I heard the tear of material — his shirt or pants, I didn't know.

"What's wrong?" I asked.

"Too fast. This is going too fast."

"What do you want, dinner and roses?"

I sat up and grabbed his belt, again yanking him toward me. I sucked on a nipple, as he tried to pull away. But I undid his belt and pants while still holding onto him.

He wasn't huge, wasn't tiny, either. As soon as I pulled him out, he groaned loudly.

I stroked him lazily, making him even bigger. I pushed down his pants and rubbed my rough five o'clock shadow against his cock. He shuddered. Just the reaction I was looking for.

I let him go, knowing that brief brush would entice him further. He'd want to feel my bristly skin against his cock, again, like super-fine sandpaper. Against his head, it would drive him wild, I knew from experience.

He panted, standing there with his pants down to his ankles, and his shirt haphazardly on his shoulders.

"Take off your clothes," he ordered.

I raised an eyebrow, and then unbuttoned my shirt, exposing my hairy, chiseled chest, and flat stomach. My denims were tented, and my dick hurt under the tight fabric.

I undid my belt and the buttons on my denims, kicking off my boots and socks, then pushed down my pants. Hairy all the way down, I was called "Bear" a few times in my life.

Artie, meanwhile, hadn't moved from his disheveled state. He stood there, watching me. I motioned to him.

"C'mon, your turn."

"I ... I just want to look."

"You want to watch me get off on you?"

He suddenly blushed like a boy on his first date.

"No one has ever been so direct about it before."

"You got them drunk first."

"Yes. Then they could think it was a drunken dream."

"Do you want me to pretend I'm drunk?"

"I — I — I don't know."

"C'mere."

I beckoned to him. He shuffled, then got out of his pants. I helped get his shirt off him. Now naked, I got him to lay down next to me. I caressed him slowly and carefully, while he actually whimpered and shuddered in my arms.

He reminded me of a boy and his first time. I wondered in all the times that he had done this before, what he did, what he had them do, whether he liked it. Whether he liked what I was doing now, caressing and kissing him slowly, doing to him what I liked having done to me, but no man in this time and place ever did.

It was always something in the closet, in the back hallways, fast and furious, without a kiss or a shudder of pleasure. I remembered a time in Greece, during the war, when men would make love on the mountainsides in full view of Selene the moon and anyone else who happened to come along. Americans were so hidden in their desires that I didn't believe it when Libra told me — but he was right.

I moved my hips closer to him and rested my cock on his thigh. I started to move my hips, rubbing my cock against him, bumping my head gently into his balls once or twice. He turned his body to face me, and moved himself so that his cock was against mine.

Then we both started to move with each other, even as I held him. I kissed his neck, nuzzled and bit, and he made the small noises of pure pleasure given by little shocks of pain. We moved, together, grinding into each other.

He moaned suddenly, a deep moan that came from the depths of his body, and I felt the wetness against my abdomen splash onto me. I kept thrusting, finally having to scoop some of him on my cock and bring myself to the edge and beyond by hand.

Artie panted like he had run a race and won, which he kind of did. He was soaked in my juices: his cock, balls and thighs. The bed was ruined.

Artie rested his head on my chest, covered in sweat. He ran his hand through my curly chest hair.

"Now, isn't it better when the guy is sober?" I asked.

"If I knew, I wouldn't have wasted my money."

I laughed. "How long are you here for?"

"One day."

"Then we better make this last."

He lifted his head. "Sleep here tonight?"

"Put down the coverlet, and I'll think about it."

4

I left at about four in the morning, even before dawn. It wouldn't do to have us both leave at the same time. People would talk. The stevedore and the actor? He was supposed to be above all that.

Artie slept with me, but he kept turning away from me in his sleep. It was a natural reaction, I thought. He probably had to sleep with a woman or two to keep up appearances, and didn't like sharing a bed with them.

I went down the street from the hotel to my room. I knew the landlord was up, because he let people in at all hours of the day and night. He never asked why, just quietly let me into the house and went back to his coffee at the kitchen table.

I never brought men back to my room. This was a very Methodist family, and just the thought of me being light in the loafers would have me out of there in ten seconds flat. I took a shower, though it was too late for that, changed clothes, and went back out with a ham sandwich for breakfast.

When I got to the theater, the rest of the guys I worked with were standing around outside. Most of them were hung over, as I expected.

"What's going on?" I asked.

"They got their own people to do the scene changes."

"So we don't work?"

"Guess not."

I looked to my supervisor, holding his head and trying to focus. Since it seemed like I was the only one sober in this group, I walked up to the door and banged on it. A few people moaned at the loud noise.

The door opened. It wasn't the theater manager, but some guy I didn't know.

"Where's Alex?"

"We don't need you," he said, and slammed the door in my face.

I banged even harder.

The supervisor said, "C'mon, forget it."

"If we're not working, I want my money from yesterday."

Now the men perked up. A couple of them joined me, banging on the door. I could have probably burst right through it, but I didn't want to show off.

Finally, Alex showed up at the door.

"Why aren't we working?" I asked.

"They brought their own guys."

"Then pay us for yesterday."

Alex sighed. "Wait right here."

We waited in the yard for about an hour, until Alex showed back up and gave us our four dollars a day. I went back around to the front of the theater and saw them setting up the marquee. Two performances tomorrow: a matinee and an evening performance.

I'd be there for one of them.

I paid the rent and went to the bar with fifty cents in my pocket, planning to buy only the cheap swill. The guys were there already, drinking the hair of the dog to get rid of their hangovers. Knowing them, they would spend their entire four dollars in the bar. There wasn't much else to do in Boise.

I spent ten cents on beer, went across the street to the theater. The box office was open.

"Hey, Mary," I said, waving to her.

"Hi, Jack!"

"How much is a ticket to the matinee tomorrow?"

"For you, a quarter."

"A whole quarter?"

"It's normally thirty-five cents."

"Nobody's going to come at that price."

"We're the only theater doing it in the area."

Disgusted, I set down my quarter. This was highway robbery.

5

That night, I waited outside of the theater for Artie. I watched as he left with some of the other actors. He paused in front of the bar, but two of the actors went in. Artie and another female actor left, going back to the hotel.

I followed, but I couldn't follow them into the hotel without being seen. I waited a few minutes, smoking a cigarette, and then I went in.

The desk clerk didn't even raise his head as I walked up to the elevators and took it to Artie's floor. I remembered the room number, and went over to the room and knocked.

Artie opened the door. He smiled, opened the door wider. I stepped inside.

I mashed his body with my own against the wall and kissed him hard. He gasped, returning the kiss.

"Well," said a man, uttering a small cough behind me.

I froze, and Artie put his hands on my chest, pushing me away gently. I turned around to see a tall, thin man sitting on the bed.

"Uh ..." Artie began.

"Scarecrow," said the man, standing up and holding out his hand to me.

I shook it, squeezing tight.

He smiled. "This isn't the first time I walked in on Artie, or Artie walked in on me, but this is the first time someone walked in on *us*."

They both had their clothes on. Artie held a stack of papers in his hand.

"Were you practicing?" I asked.

"Just leaving," said Scarecrow.

"No," I said.

Scarecrow raised an eyebrow. "No?"

I gazed at Artie. "What do you think?"

Artie blushed furiously.

Scarecrow bolted the door and locked it. "This," he said, "should be very interesting."

"I don't know," said Artie, as Scarecrow came up behind him.

I came up to his front, pressing my body against him again, and Scarecrow pressed himself against Artie's back. Scarecrow's hand caressed my arm as his other hand rubbed Artie's arm.

"Oh, my God," Artie whispered. "We're going to get in —"

"No, we won't," said Scarecrow.

He was taller than Artie, about my height. He leaned forward and Artie tilted his head to the side, letting the man kiss me.

He was a pretty good kisser, I'll admit that. Artie kissed like a scared colt, but this guy, he kissed like he had all the time in the world.

One of my hands went down to Artie's butt and squeezed, while my other hand snaked around to Scarecrow's ass and also squeezed. Both men gasped, as Scarecrow jerked forward.

I looked at Scarecrow. "I'm going to butt-fuck him."

"By all means, sir," said Scarecrow. "And he can suck me."

"Deal," I replied, and started to strip Artie of his clothes.

Scarecrow helped, pulling off his shirt, his pants, his shoes and socks. Artie didn't know where to turn, but both Scarecrow and I divested ourselves of our clothes, while Artie watched.

"Do you have any juice?" I asked Artie.

"Suitcase."

I found the aluminum tube of petroleum jelly. But before I could get that started, Scarecrow had bent down and kissed Artie's ass, dragging his tongue through the crack. Artie moaned loudly. I sat on the bed, watching Scarecrow drive his face far into Artie's soft ass, spreading it wide, and preparing it for me.

Artie was a quivering mass at this point.

Scarecrow finally got up, grinning, his face glistening with saliva. "All ready for you, sir."

I grinned, grabbed Artie by the waist, and yanked him to me. I got up from the bed, and guided Artie to face the bed. He put his hands on the edge of the bed, while Scarecrow climbed onto the bed and shoved his cock in Artie's face.

Just watching that made me harder, and I smeared jelly all over my cock, then into his hole, which had been stretched by Scarecrow's tongue. I pushed forward, sliding easily into him.

Artie, his mouth stuffed with Scarecrow's cock, could only make a high-pitched noise that could have been a scream of pain or pleasure. I honestly didn't care which; I drove myself into him, slamming him hard.

His body moved on its own, back and forth, me directing his body's rhythm while he sucked Scarecrow. Scarecrow had wiped his face, leaning in for a kiss. I bent my head, concentrating on Artie.

I grabbed Artie's cock and started stroking it while he screamed again. He started making small sounds of pleasure as I pounded into him, stroked him, and watched him take Scarecrow down.

Scarecrow exploded first, pulling back and shooting all over Artie's back, some as far as his ass, leaking down his crack. I didn't stop, but watching it made me more hot.

Then Artie shot all along the edge of the bed, covering my hand. That pushed me over the edge. I growled and shot my load into him, overflowing him, dripping onto the carpet.

"God damn," said Scarecrow, leaning back onto the bed.

Artie collapsed on the floor, yanking me out of him. I leaned against the wall, looking at the mess before me.

"Next town," said Scarecrow, "I'm gonna fuck you, Artie."

"Next town," I said, "I'm gonna fuck *you*, Scarecrow."

"How's that?"

"You're gonna need a stevedore." I walked over and grabbed my pants. "I'll make sure of it."

6

The matinee was crowded with kids and people, probably from most of the state. Wagons and cars were lined up and down the street downtown. I wore my usual work clothes.

I showed them my ticket and one of the ushers I knew showed me to my seat. It was next to a family, everyone wearing their Sunday best. I didn't really have a Sunday best. They gave me a condescending look, wondering why in the world one man would want to see *The Wonderful*

Wizard of Oz. I didn't want to see the play; I wanted to see the Cowardly Lion.

The play started, the orchestra played, and I watched the scene changes.

Very well done, I thought, knowing what I had to do.

The Scarecrow had a booming, belting voice that echoed beautifully through the theater. Then came Artie. I was disappointed, because he was in a mask to look like the Lion. But he was smaller than everyone, except Dorothy and the Little People.

I knew how they did the fogs, the fires, and flying. The kids next to me didn't, though, and they gasped and screamed at each effect. I laughed at their antics. Although I could tell them how it was done, I didn't want to ruin their good time.

Then the last song was sung by the entire cast, the lights came up, and the magic was over.

I sat in my seat and waited for people to leave, then I approached the stage.

One of the stage hands stopped me. It was a man I didn't know. "No one's allowed back here."

"I work here."

"Not today you don't."

Here was my chance. I could make the decision and ruin this man's life for my own success. It wasn't a hard decision.

I shoved him. He fell off the stage and into the orchestra pit, landing hard on his leg. Along with a loud bang of some instruments getting knocked over, I thought I heard the snap of bone.

I looked up to see three men come running when they heard the crash of a body on instruments.

"He fell," I said to the men. "Looks like you need a new scene-changer."

SAGITTARIUS

WASHINGTON D.C.
MARCH 30, 1981

I

PROTECTING THE PRESIDENT WAS, in Rory's opinion, the most boring job in the world. He'd had a few doozies: Agincourt archer, captain of the walls in Fort Ticonderoga, a trick-rider in a carnival. But being a "crow", a sniper in the building far above where the President was going to come out, was too redundant.

There were three crows; the other two had spotters. Rory was just that damn good that he didn't need a spotter.

The President came out of the back door of the hotel. Rory settled in, looking through the scope. He didn't see anything amiss.

Until the crowd scattered.

He swept across the area, the reflections in the scope blurs. *Where was he? Where was the shooter?*

He saw a pile of Secret Service men on the ground, and kept his eye on that.

"Rawhide down," he heard in his earpiece.

Shit, Rory thought.

Someone had shot the President.

2

Rory went back to the office, disappointed and angry like the rest of the men. The President was in surgery. No one knew what to think, if he would survive or not. He was in his 70s, after all.

"I didn't see him," Rory heard Carl say when he walked into the conference room. "Nobody saw him."

Carl was one of the spotters. The two crows and their spotters were, along with their supervisor, Jesus D'Orio. They called him Grumpy Cat behind his back, because he wore a perpetual scowl.

Today was no exception. D'Orio stood at the head of the table while Rory took a seat toward the back.

"I saw who it was after they jumped him," said one of the crows.

D'Orio looked directly at Rory. "You were closest."

"I didn't see anything until after."

"We're getting you a spotter."

Rory slapped his palm on the table. "C'mon, you know I don't need one." *I've been doing this kind of thing for over five hundred years,* he wanted to blurt out.

"You're getting a spotter and that's final. You're not all that special."

The other two crows didn't look at him, but they had slight grins. Rory *was* that special, and the rest of the team was jealous. To see him dressed down and treated like the rest of the team probably made them feel better.

Rory put up token resistance. He didn't need a spotter, and knew that he didn't have to pay attention to the spotter if he felt like it.

"So bring in some kid just out of marksman school to fill in the job, I don't care."

"You'll see," said D'Orio. "Dismissed."

The men all got up and went out into the main room. There, they could see on TV, ran a replay of the actual shooting.

There's no way I could have seen that, Rory thought.

Rory went to his desk, which faced one of the TV's. Unlike those of his teammates, his desk held only the awards he had gotten from many competitions; no pictures of girlfriends or family to inspire him throughout the day. The awards didn't inspire him much, either.

He just loved his job. Well, if, in order to keep it, he had to play by the rules, he would act like it. It didn't mean he was going to *play* by their rules.

3

Rory left late, in an effort to avoid the crowded Metro. It worked, for the most part; the staffers and government workers had mostly gone home. His apartment was two rooms in a boarding house with a bathroom shared by four other men. One he knew well; the other three were passing acquaintances.

The TV was on in the main lobby, playing more about the assassination attempt. The suspect was named John Hinkley Jr.. Not much was known about him. Rory knew his cohorts in the FBI would find out soon enough — if not already.

His two rooms were cluttered. The main room had a desk and chair, a well-used winged-back chair he claimed from an old tenant, and books. Everywhere, in every corner, there were books. Books on history, religion, current events, biographies, war, peace, fiction, and best sellers. He picked up books on anything and everything.

Rory organized them all, at least in his head. This pile was the Vietnam war. This pile was the Civil War that he had participated in, how they had gotten some facts wrong about his battalion. The other pile was about the Confederacy that he fought against.

Then there was the pile next to his bed in the other room. Those were ones he hadn't read yet. Okay, so there was more than one pile of those. But he'd get to them.

He took off his jacket and tossed it in the pile that was his laundry. He'd have to get that done soon; he was down to one jacket, two pairs of pants, and two shirts. *Maybe tonight,* he thought, *I'll stake out the laundry room with the biography of Katherine Hepburn.*

A knock came at his door. He opened it to see Jake, one of the men he shared the bathroom with.

"Hey, did you hear what happened?" Jake asked, stepping into the room.

"Yeah," said Rory. "I was there."

"No shit."

Rory nodded. "Couldn't see the shooter. There were too many people around."

Jake was a small man; an auditor for the Department of Interior, on the other side of the city. Sometimes Rory caught Jake on the Metro and they'd walk back home together, but those times were rare. Jake wore contacts that kept popping out of his hazel eyes; Rory knew that Jake had reading glasses in addition to the contacts.

"What's for dinner?"

"Ravioli." Although they weren't allowed to have hot plates in their rooms, everyone did. However, Rory had learned to eat ravioli cold out of the can.

"Want to go out?"

"Are you asking me on a date?"

Jake chuckled like he always did when they shared that common joke.

"Damn you, you get me every time."

"I can go out. Let me get changed."

"Ok. See you downstairs in ten."

Rory got out a t-shirt and jeans, pulled on his denim jacket and slipped into his Converses, his only brand loyalty. Meeting Jake downstairs, they stepped outside, away from the smoke in the lobby.

"Where to?" asked Rory.

"You know what I really want? Chicago deep-dish pizza."

Rory laughed. "In this town? You're gonna have to settle for Domino's."

"There's a place a few stops up the Metro. I heard one of the guys talking about it."

"Okay, let's go on an adventure."

4

Rory couldn't escape the assassination attempt news. Everyone was talking about it, and it was on all the TV's.

Jake sat back with his beer. "Not bad, huh?"

"I've had better in New Jersey." *In 1930* — but he didn't dare mention that.

"Connoisseur."

Rory shrugged. "You can't find good food in this town. It's all gentrified."

Jake raised his beer. "But the beer is cold."

"That's not that great, either."

"Killjoy. What's wrong with you?"

"Sick of hearing about the assassination attempt, to be honest."

"It's not your fault."

"I would have had a clear shot if people didn't get in the way."

"See? It's not your fault."

Rory drank his dark beer, something that was close to real beer, not the piss of Budweiser. "It was easier in the Army."

"Because you had targets that stood still."

"Not necessarily."

He didn't have a spotter in the Army, either. Rory realized what was really bothering him.

"They're giving me a babysitter."

"What do you mean?"

"They're giving me a spotter. Some snipers need someone to look around the area to make sure the target is clear." He frowned. "They're babysitters. Like I can't tell what's going on around me."

"Maybe they're trying to help."

Rory snorted. "I'll have to protect him, too."

"I'm sure he can protect himself. You're all ex-Armed Forces guys, right? For all you know, he might be some big Marine who can take anyone down by using his pinky."

Rook laughed, and thought, *That could be damn interesting.*

5

Tuesday, and the office was still reeling from the assassination attempt. Rory figured he was going to be in his suit all day because the president was still in the hospital. He'd be there for a few days, most likely, due to his age and how close the bullet came to killing him.

He turned the corner to his desk to see a man sitting in his chair, his feet up on his desk. He wore a dark suit like the rest of them, but with a skull-and-crossbones design on his tie. His brown hair was short. He was clean-shaven, and his dark blue eyes held a bit of mischievousness to them.

He wasn't the big Marine that Jake had envisioned; instead, he was trim and well-built. Rory wouldn't throw him out of bed for eating crackers.

"Good morning, Mr. Taggart," he said, his voice holding a midwestern accent.

"And you are?"

He took his feet down from the desk, and fluidly stood up. "Special Agent Nicholas Carlito." He held out his hand. "Everyone calls me Nick."

Rory shook the hand, a firm, dry handshake. *Good,* Rory thought.

"Where you from?"

"FBI."

"I didn't do anything," Rory said immediately.

"I transferred from the FBI."

"Oh."

"I'm supposed to be working with you."

"Nobody told me any —"

"I see you've met your spotter," said Rory's boss, D'Orio, coming around the corner. "Carlito, Taggert —"

"We've been introduced," said Rory quickly.

Carlito smiled. "Nice guy," he said, thumbing at Rory.

D'Orio snorted. "Go get dressed. The Vice President is going to make a speech. I just need one team there, and you're going."

"Yes, sir," they both said.

"You know where you're going?" asked Rory.

"Locker room downstairs," Nick replied.

"So you're not new here."

"I was a pencil pusher for a while until they decided what to do with me."

"You've never done spotting before?"

"How hard can it be?"

Rory held back a sharp "Jesus Christ" that was aimed at D'Orio.

"You're responsible for me," Rory said. "And everything that's around the target."

"Like I said, how hard can it be?"

"You'll see."

6

The Vice President was speaking indoors, in lieu of the president, so they were placed on the roof near the main entrance. Rory was pointing straight down, into a draw as the Army would term it. Not the perfect place, but the only one they could get on such short notice.

Security was beefed up to a crazy degree. The Vice President was absolutely surrounded by big, beefy Secret Security men. He couldn't move without bumping into the guys. Nick had binoculars and watched the movement below. He instinctively scanned around him.

Maybe he doesn't need training, Rory thought.

The Vice President came out, crowded by the Secret Service agents. Nothing was going to get by them; nothing did.

"Clear," said Nick, as the car pulled away.

Rory had the habit of keeping the car in his sights until he knew he no longer had the range, and then he relaxed. He looked up from the scope to see Nick watching him. Actually ... watching his butt.

Rory smiled and started to get up. Nick gave him a hand up.

"Well, that was easy," Nick said.

"You've never spotted before?"

"Nope." He grinned. "How did I do?"

"Okay, I guess."

"You think you don't need a spotter, huh?"

Rory plucked at his Kevlar. "Yeah, well, I've been doing this for years."

"Right, old man," Nick said, and helped to gather the equipment.

Rory would normally wince at being called an "old man", but this time, he didn't seem to mind.

7

The next few days were uneventful. The President was still in recovery, the Vice-President kept his outings to a minimum, and things settled down in the office.

One Monday morning, Nick didn't show up at Rory's desk at the usual nine o'clock hour, so Rory went looking for him.

With some direction, he found Nick's desk, and was surprised.

On his desk were marksmanship awards from the FBI. He wasn't a sniper, but he was a damn good shot: winning gold in some awards, silver in others. Rory went to D'Orio's office.

"Nick out today?"

D'Orio jerked his head up from looking at the computer. "What?"

"Nick. Is he out today?"

"Yeah. PTO. Catch up on your firewall exams or something."

Rory went back to Nick's desk for another once-over, this time looking for any pictures. Just like his own, there were no pictures of him with other people. There was a picture of a young man in an Air Force uniform, a picture of him with a woman in a pink dress, but she looked similar to Nick, so it could have been a sister. That same woman was in a family photo with an older man and woman. *Yep, a sister.*

He decided he'd broach the subject of whether or not Nick was divorced. Up on a roof, it was only them. It could only be between them. Although Rory had been through this kind of thing for years, he usually could tell which way the wind blew for most men.

The next day, Nick was at his desk. He had a bruise under his left eye.

"What happened?" Rory asked, pointing to his own cheek.

Nick just shook his head. "Don't want to go into it. We're going to California."

"We are?"

"Did you check your email?"

"I just got in. What do you do, live here?"

"Technically, no. But I spend enough time here to justify paying rent if I have to."

Rory snorted and shooed Nick out of his chair. He smelled like Polo.

"Let me check the computer." Rory signed into his account and noted the email.

He and Nick were going to be Alpha team outside of a ranch in California while the President convalesced. But first, they had to go out and scope the place for other sniper spots.

"Guess I better go home and pack."

"Where do you live?"

"Manassas."

"I'm out that way, too. We can share a taxi."

Rory raised an eyebrow. "You've got money for a taxi?"

"It's a splurge. I take the Metro like you do."

"How do you know I take the Metro?"

"You don't go in the parking garage when you get out."

"Are you following me?" asked Rory.

Nick sipped his coffee in the paper cup. "Taxi?"

"Yeah, sure, I guess."

"I'll pick you up for the airport. How long do you need?"

"An hour."

"Sounds good." Nick turned around and left. Rory had the niggling feeling that something was going to happen.

The taxi trip was uneventful, though Nick sat close to the window. Rory's house was first, so he got out in front of the brownstone that was his rooming house.

"I'll be back at noon," said Nick, which gave him two hours to pack.

Nick had to go to his house and pack, also, then drive back through the traffic to pick him up.

Rory packed the bare essentials, thinking he was only going to be there for a couple of days. It was a scouting mission, which meant a day, maybe two. Enough for only a carry-on.

Nick picked him up about ten past noon. He drove a silver Escort. Rory was happy that he drove a newer car than his ancient Volkswagen that he had bought new in 1969.

"Sorry, traffic is a bear. We're going to Andrews?"

"Yeah," said Rory, as Nick pulled out into traffic.

Andrews Air Force Base would provide them with a military plane along with the other secret service men who were going to scope out the ranch.

"We've got until three, anyway," said Nick. "Which will probably be just enough time for us to get there."

They got through the Beltway traffic and headed toward the base. Rory knew that now would be the perfect time to ask.

"So, hey, I was wondering."

"Yeah?"

"You, um ... divorced?"

Nick stiffened a moment. "Why do you say that?"

"I didn't see any wedding pictures on your desk."

"No, not divorced."

"Seeing anyone?"

He shrugged. "You might say that."

"Oh," said Rory, looking away.

"It's not working out," said Nick. "We live together. Fight all the time."

"That's where the —"

"Yeah."

"She must've got you good."

He swallowed. That's when Rory knew.

"Listen," said Rory, "Don't tell anyone, but —?"

Nick said, "I already know."

At a stop light, they looked at each other. Eye to eye, soul to soul. They were both the same.

Nick nodded, and the light changed.

So did everything else.

8

Rory knew to put his sexual wants aside when it came to his job. He joined the other men in the military plane that was headed to California.

When they arrived, the ranch that they found was sprawling, open land with a couple of buildings that gave the Secret Service agents conniptions.

"Anyone here can ride a horse?" asked Agent Foss, the leader.

Rory looked around and sheepishly raised his hand.

"You lead when he goes out horseback riding."

"Yes, sir," said Rory.

Nick raised an eyebrow. "Horseback riding?"

Rory shrugged. "Parents, you know?"

"Uh huh."

"Go take a look at the trails," ordered Foss.

Rory went into the stable and asked for a horse. They saddled a quiet mare named Tina. Rory borrowed a pair of cowboy boots and rode out into the fields.

He examined the trails, went into the woods on foot, looking at the deer and rabbit trails, the areas around him, where they could place men. He noted when the trail could only walk one at a time, so they would have to cut some trees to make it wider. Some brush would need to be cleared, also.

By the time he got back, he was covered in sweat, leaves, twigs, and burrs. Although the rest of the team laughed at him, Foss was hungry for the information that he had. In one of the small cottages on the property, they mapped out the trails while eating lunch. Nick had gone to scope out the property for sniper placement.

"Don't put me on horseback the whole time," Rory pleaded to Foss.

"Only when he goes out, which probably won't be this time around."

"You never know with him. He's a tough guy."

Foss chuckled. "That, he is. We'll get volunteers, okay?"

Nick returned with the other agents, and one of them gave a report. Nick reported on the sniper placements, though Rory wanted to go check them out himself. It wasn't that he didn't trust Nick; it's just that Rory had done this kind of thing so often that he knew instinctively where to place people.

He had to let it go. He was on horse detail now.

9

They made it back to the hotel at ten at night. Of course, Rory and Nick bunked together.

They got to their room. Rory divested himself of his sweat-stained jacket and shirt, while Nick watched from the bed.

"Before anything, I need a shower."

"Need any help with that?" asked Nick with a mischievous grin.

"Depends. Do you need a shower?"

"A cold one," Nick said, passing his hand along his abs. Rory knew what that signaled.

"I usually take hot showers."

"All the better with two," said Nick, getting out of his shirt. He was more hairy than Rory — thick Italian black hair along his chest.

Rory wasn't even thinking, *Are you sure we should do this?* It had happened too many times to count, where he worked with the same people he fucked. To him, it was a fun thing; though maybe to others, it was serious. He couldn't tell if Nick was serious until the moment Nick got up from the bed and kissed him.

That kiss was more than lust.

Rory tried to say to himself, *It's only for fun, nothing serious.*

Nick pulled away, nibbling at Rory's lower lip when he did. Rory shivered, his nipples hardening immediately.

Nick ignored — or enjoyed — the sweaty smell of him as he bent to lick those diamond points on Rory's chest. Rory cast his head back, as Nick's tongue flicked the nipple, and the feeling of it went right to his dick.

"Stop, Jesus."

Nick lifted his head. "Am I doing something wrong?"

Rory pressed his crotch against Nick's. It bulged just as much.

Rory got undressed in front of Nick. Nick fumbled with his own belt, and Rory, grinning, helped him. Now naked, they stared at each other, studying each other. Both were well-built; Rory with muscular shoulders from all those years at Agincourt. The Goddess Ishtar had plucked him at his prime.

Nick was thinner, with a runner's body, lithe and hairy, though. Rory wasn't sure which way this was going to go, but he was flexible. A Mutable sign.

Rory took Nick by the hand and pulled him into the bathroom. He bent over to put on the shower, and Nick pressed his crotch against his ass.

So, this was how it was going to go, he thought, and smiled as he turned on the water.

Then came a knock on the door.

"Shit!" hissed Nick.

"You answer it."

"Fuck," Nick said, and went back out into the room. With a chuckle, Rory jumped into the shower.

"Ah, m'Lady, you are amusing," he said quietly in Gaelic as he used the tiny hotel soap bar to lather up.

Nick pushed aside the curtain a few seconds after Rory finished washing his hair. "Foss wanted you."

"I thought you did."

"I do, but he wants you first."

"Aw, hell." Rory got out of the shower.

Nick stood with a towel, holding it open. Rory let Nick dry him off. Nick rubbed all the places he himself wanted to be touched, leaving his extended cock and low-hanging balls for last.

"You're an awful tease," Rory said.

"I've heard that before," Nick replied, swatting Rory on the butt. "Go get dressed before Foss wonders if I've ravished you."

"He wouldn't be wrong."

Rory went up to Foss's hotel room and knocked on the door. He was brought inside. Foss and three other men were gathered around a cardboard diorama of the ranch. It included land that wasn't part of the ranch, but was either public land or part of another person's land.

Cut into the diorama were the trails based on Rory's map. For three more hours, they discussed modifications, fortifications, and placements of men and checkpoints. Foss dismissed them a little after three in the morning. The men stumbled back to their rooms to try and catch three hours' sleep.

When Rory got back, Nick was fast asleep on the bed. Rory collapsed on his bed and passed out until the hotel desk called them at six.

IO

"Why do I feel like shit and you look fine?" asked Nick as he hung his head over the coffee in the diner.

Rory laughed. "Because I've done this for a long time. I can live on bits of sleep for about a month."

"Hell," said Nick, drinking the hot mud of a coffee. "You'd think they'd be able to make a decent cup of coffee."

"Well, they screwed up the breakfast, what else do you expect?"

Rory had ordered no hash browns. He got them delivered on his plate anyway. He had passed them off to Nick.

Rory hoped they wouldn't be here another day. He didn't have the clothes for it, for one, and, for another, he wanted to make sure Nick was not on the rebound because of his boyfriend troubles. At least, that's what Rory was saying to himself.

He'd dreamed that the two of them, older and in tuxes, stood in front of a desk, with two other men beside them. Rory and Nick held hands, and recited words that Rory never said in this context during all his years: "I do."

Rory knew from the dream that the Lady Ishtar was sending him a pretty clear message. He accepted that, but he wanted to make sure. He was used to the fun of the chase, but once he had the man he wanted, it was boring. Would it be different with Nick?

Rory was back on sniper duty, verifying the places that Nick had chosen. For the area, they were adequate, but needed some extra fortification. He suggested a watchtower at a certain point, but Foss said that would cost too much, and the President would never go for it.

As for the horseback riding, Rory was going to be lead on that, even though Foss said he sent an email to all the agents that had horse training to get "voluntolds", volunteers who were, more or less, given orders to participate.

When Rory and Nick finally got together, it was to head back to Washington D.C. on a military plane. Five other men were with them.

Rory was already a member of the Mile-High Club, and decided to try and initiate Nick into it. The five men settled down to sleep the six hours it was going to take to get them back to Washington.

Nick also settled back, Rory sitting next to him. They were sitting across from three men, asleep. Rory placed his hand on Nick's thigh, and started rubbing up and down the inside of his leg.

Nick stirred, automatically opened his legs. Rory kept rubbing upward, bumping against his crotch once or twice. Nick grunted each time. When Rory finally cupped Nick's crotch, Nick snapped his eyes open.

"Are you crazy?" he whispered.

"Yep," Rory said, squeezing his hardening member.

"The guys," Nick, said, as Rory ticked down Nick's zipper.

"So? They're asleep."

"They might hear."

"Then keep quiet," Rory said, again palming Nick's cock.

He pulled it out of his pants, and was satisfied with its size and thickness. It would feel good inside him, Rory thought, and he'd feel good inside Nick.

Rory stroked him slowly, getting him thicker and harder. Nick took long, deep breaths in rhythm with the strokes. Rory knew he had him, so he stroked faster. Nick kept looking around, watching for the other guys to see if they were awake and watching. If they were awake, they didn't show it.

"Fuck," Nick whispered.

"Okay," said Rory, and stopped stroking for a moment. He stood up in the plane. The plane was high enough for him to stand up straight, and pull down his pants.

"Are you fucking crazy?"

Rory just gave him a grin and stepped one leg out of his pants. He knelt on the wide bench they sat on, and he squeezed out pre-cum from Nick. It was barely enough; it was going to hurt, but Rory didn't care.

Nick spurted a little, which was enough to coat his hole. Nick's eyes were wide and scared as Rory slowly lowered himself onto Nick's cock. Rory didn't make a sound, but Nick moaned, caught himself, and bit his lip to stop himself from making any more noise.

Rory raised and lowered himself, not caring where they were, not caring that there may be five men watching them. *Good for them if they were,* Rory thought, as he rode Nick.

Nick gripped the side of the bench and thrust up whenever Rory came down. He could only do it a few times before he said, "Man, I'm —"

Rory put a finger on Nick's lips. "Shhh."

Nick's breathing got faster, shallower. Then he closed his eyes, cast his head back, and closed his mouth tight. The moan came from his chest, reverberating throughout his body. Rory stopped and clenched his ass around Nick, milking him for everything he had.

After a minute, when Nick's breathing slowed to normal, Rory disengaged and stood up, pulling on his pants.

"You pass. Now get some sleep," Rory said, as he sat on the bench next to Nick. He folded his hands under his head for a pillow and pretended to go to sleep.

Nick finally got himself together and did the same thing.

II

They arrived back at Washington DC at six in the morning. They were still expected to go into the office. Rory got the largest cup of coffee he could find and went to his desk. He didn't look tired, but he sure as hell felt it.

He went to visit Nick, who was not in much better shape. He had skipped the coffee altogether and gotten himself an espresso from the cafe downstairs.

"I can smell that all the way to my desk," Rory said as Nick sat hunched over the espresso.

"You kept me awake all night."

"I did no such thing."

Nick tilted his head and gave Rory an "Are you kidding me?" look.

"I've got an idea. Let's bunk."

"Bunk?"

Rory leaned in. "Didn't you ever bunk school? Skip a day?"

Nick looked around again.

"Nobody cares if we take the day off. In fact, if you come to my place, I'll get you lunch."

Nick swallowed. "I'll call you tomorrow."

Rory smiled. He went back to his desk and the rest of the day passed slowly. He knew he was going to crash tonight.

Jake wasn't around that day, it seemed, so he ate his ravioli out of the can. He wondered, fleetingly, whether Nick would mind the mess that his room was in, with books tossed everywhere. He at least had to clear the books off the bed.

Rory's alarm went off at five. He turned over in bed and called sick into work. After he came out of the bathroom, his phone rang.

"Hello?" he asked.

"Hey," whispered Nick.

Rory grinned. "Did you?"

"Yeah."

"Come over."

"After nine."

Ah, the boyfriend. Nick hung up without saying goodbye. Rory lay back on the bed, tucked his hands under his head and stared up at the cracked ceiling.

He had a feeling, just a feeling, that this was his last incarnation, and that Nick Carlito was his final lover.

He smiled. "Thank you, m'Lady," he whispered to the ceiling.

YOU MIGHT ALSO ENJOY

Earth
A Brothers of the Zodiac Collection
by Maxwell Thomas

Three stories of the Earth signs: Capricorn, Taurus, and Virgo.

Water
A Brothers of the Zodiac Collection
by Maxwell Thomas

Three Stories of the Water signs: Aries, Leo, and Sagittarius.

Available from Zarra Knightley Publishing
in trade paperback, digital, and audio editions.

zarraknightleypublishing.com

www.ingramcontent.com/pod-product-compliance
Lightning Source LLC
Chambersburg PA
CBHW022041170626
46808CB00003B/1310